Ready to Write a Book?

Do you collect images of your town or county? Are you passionate about local history, and eager to share what you've learned? If you or your organization always dreamed of writing a book, we would love to hear from you. We are eagerly seeking authors to write illustrated, regional history and guide books. We'd love to hear more about the images you have access to, and the audience you are writing for.

Email your book idea to info@schifferbooks.com, write to Acquisitions, Schiffer Publishing, Ltd. 4880 Lower Valley Rd., Atglen, PA 19310 USA, or call 610-593-1777 to make an appointment to speak with an editor.

The Sand Lady

AN OCEAN CITY MARYLAND TALE

CORINNE M. LITZENBERG
ILLUSTRATIONS BY
BARI A. EDWARDS

Schiffer Publishing Ltd

4880 Lower Valley Road, Atglen, Pennsylvania 19310

Other Schiffer Books by Corinne M. Litzenberg
The Sand Lady: A Cape May Tale.

Other Schiffer Books on Related Subjects
Wading & Shore Birds of the Atlantic Coast.
    Roger S. Everett
Upper Chesapeake Bay Decoys and Their Makers.
    David & Joan Hagan

Maryland Blue Crab

Designed by "Sue"
Type set in Americana XBd BT/Zurich BT
ISBN: 978-0-7643-2684-4
Printed in China

Published by Schiffer Publishing Ltd.
4880 Lower Valley Road
Atglen, PA 19310
Phone: (610) 593-1777; Fax: (610) 593-2002
E-mail: Info@schifferbooks.com

For the largest selection of fine reference books on this and related subjects, please visit our web site at www.schifferbooks.com
We are always looking for people to write books on new and related subjects. If you have an idea for a book please contact us at the above address.

This book may be purchased from the publisher.
Include $3.95 for shipping.
Please try your bookstore first.
You may write for a free catalog.

In Europe, Schiffer books are distributed by
Bushwood Books
6 Marksbury Ave.
Kew Gardens
Surrey TW9 4JF England
Phone: 44 (0) 20 8392-8585; Fax: 44 (0) 20 8392-9876
E-mail: info@bushwoodbooks.co.uk
Website: www.bushwoodbooks.co.uk
Free postage in the U.K., Europe; air mail at cost.

DEDICATION

For Todd and Natalie, Jenny and Jillian, Madeleine and Melanie, and Sarah and Seth
—C. L.

Baltimore
Checkerspot
Butterfly

ILLUSTRATOR DEDICATION

For Rachelle Nicole Katz, Amanda Bryn Katz, and Arianna Marie Minnick
—B. E.

CONTENTS

Old Ocean City, MD
c 1912

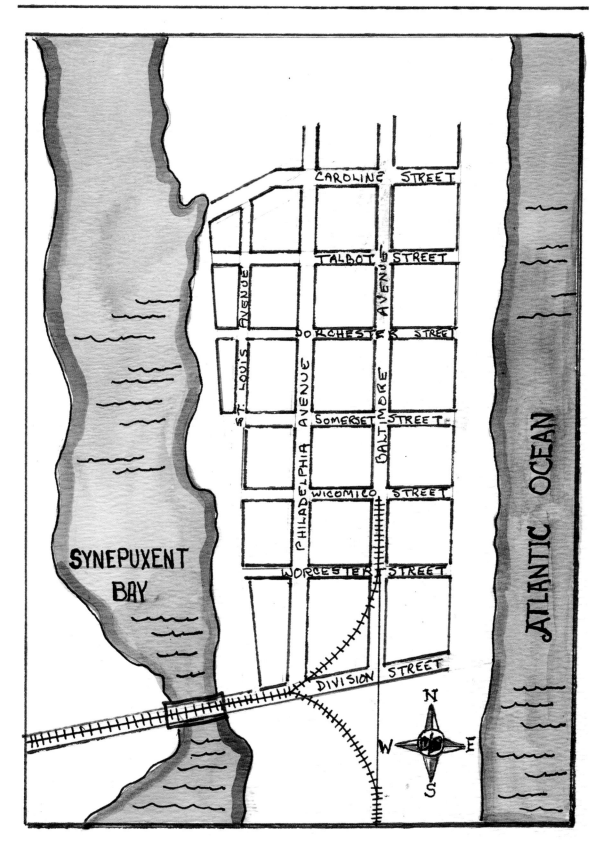

Summer Vacation

Beth Williams sipped on her tea and peered out the bay window, watching as her daughter, Jillian, climbed up the porch steps. Cradled in her wet tee shirt were shells: razor clams, oysters, and a few mussels.

"Now don't bring all that sand in here. Put your shells on the deck and shake out your shirt," her mother said.

Jillian admired each shell as she placed them in a row.

She called through the screen, "When's Dad getting back? You said we could fly kites today!"

"He should be home soon," her mother answered.

Jillian's father had been on a fishing trip with some of his friends. Every year in early June, the same group of watermen met for their annual fishing tournament on the Sinepuxent Bay at Talbot Street. They would charter a deep sea fishing boat for offshore fishing to see who could catch the biggest fish. Each year, Jillian looked forward to her father's return. He was always bringing her back something: a hermit crab, pretty shells, and once a real starfish. There was always fresh fish for dinner, such as bluefish, sea trout, rockfish or tuna. She would watch her dad clean the fish as they talked about their day.

It was during these summer vacation mornings in Ocean City that Beth would sit at her easel near the bay window and paint watercolor seascapes and lighthouses. She enjoyed taking photographs on their summer vacations and painting scenes in watercolor from their trip. Beth was able to frame and sell her artwork at local art festivals.

Her husband, Richard, loved to fish.

He would always say, "A bad day's fishin' beats a good day's workin'."

This is the way their summers began. Jillian's mom came to paint, and her dad came to fish. For once, they forgot about their daily, hectic lives of office work, car pools, and housework. During the rest of the year, watercolor painting and fishing were always placed on the backburner. There were never enough hours in a day for their true pastimes until summer.

"Before he gets here, why don't you take Sable for a w-a-l-k?" her mother suggested. "She hasn't been out all morning."

Sable was the family's black lab. She demanded each family member's attention and understood every spoken word. She wagged her tail and barked sharply at Jill, then retrieved her red, nylon leash from the pantry. Sable thrashed the leash about wildly. The metal hook clanged against the refrigerator. She dropped the leash from her mouth and pounced on it with her front paws.

"Look, Mom. Sable's learned how to spell, too!" said Jillian. "Okay, already, okay, we'll go," Jillian assured her.

Sable tried to be patient. The black lab's tail swept the floor and her pink tongue lolled below her white bearded chin. She nosed herself partway out the screen door. Jillian managed to snag her collar with the leash's hook and pull her back firmly before Sable could bolt down to the beach. After all, "chasing Sable" was Sable's favorite game! Sable obeyed and loped by Jillian's side down Bunting Avenue.

Beth managed to get in a solid hour of painting when she heard the screen door slap shut.

"Guess what's for supper?" her husband announced cheerfully as he presented her with a white, plastic bucket of fresh rockfish. "Where's our girl?" he added.

Beth looked up at the clock on the stove, "Oh, you know Jillian. She's off wandering down the beach with Sable. I'm sure she'll be home when she gets hungry."

Richard scratched the sand from his ear, "Easy catchin' today. Jerry caught the biggest sea bass ... must've weighed fifty pounds. He could hardly reel 'em in."

"I just brewed a fresh pot of iced tea. There's still some pie left. Why don't you rest a bit?" she suggested.

Beth leaned against the kitchen counter, took a sip of her iced tea and sighed deeply.

"Richard, Jillian asked me to fly kites with her again. I told her several times that as soon as I had this last painting finished I would have more time to spend with her. Jilly just has to be a little more patient," she explained.

Beth reached for a glass from the cupboard and set it on the counter. She poured her husband a cup of iced tea and waited for a response.

"I know, Beth," he replied. "I don't know what the answer is. We just got down here."

"Say," he thought, "There's a community bonfire on the beach tonight. Why don't the three of us go? It would be fun."

Richard put his arms around his wife's waist.

"And I promise I won't tell the story about the dune monster," Richard said as he growled in Beth's ear in a playful way.

Jillian's father was quite the storyteller at family picnics, and he could tell some whoppers.

"Sounds like a great idea to me," Beth agreed. "I'll pack the bug spray."

The Sirman Cottage, Fenwick Island, Delaware.

6

FENWICK ISLAND

Jillian and Sable walked down Bunting Avenue. From afar, she could see the tall tower of the Fenwick Lighthouse on the other side of Coastal Highway, the highest point on Fenwick Island. The midday sun hung high as noisy sea gulls soared toward the Atlantic. Sable barked at a turtle crossing the road. The turtle quickly poked her head and feet inside her protective shell. Jillian recognized the diamond-shaped shell as a *Diamondback Terrapin.* From May through July, female turtles would lay their eggs on the shores of the coastal bays. Once in a while, Jillian would find a turtle on her walks with Sable. She carefully picked the turtle up and moved her to the other side of the road, so she could make her way to the bay. She felt self-rewarded doing this. It was her way of helping the environment and her favorite ecosystems, the bay and the ocean.

After their walk, Jillian tied Sable near the crepe myrtle tree in the sandy backyard of their family cottage and gave her a cold bowl of water from the hose. Jillian headed down to the ocean water's edge to wade her feet and collect some more shells.

Jillian toted her sea treasures in her shirt back to her favorite thinking spot near their summer cottage. Under the shady, pink crepe myrtle tree she began to sort through her shells. The sand felt cool. Perfect for making sandcastles. With her finger, she wrote her name in cursive. Jillian sighed. She was tired of spending her family vacation alone. She wished her mother would finish her painting and fly kites on the beach like they planned. Her Dad promised he would take her to Assateague Island to see the wild ponies. They talked about playing miniature golf and going to Frontier Town to pan for gold and ride the waterslide. She was feeling sorry for herself. Couldn't her mother find somewhere else inspiring to paint? They were both imposing on *her* family vacation time. Now that they were finally down in Ocean City, when were they going to spend time with *her*? Jillian sulked. She felt her parents … and adults in general for that matter … just did not care much what kids thought.

Diamondback Terrapin Turtle.

Assateague Island Horse.

THE SAND LADY

In her secret spot, Jillian rubbed Sable behind her ears and spoke lovingly to her, "You're a good girl, oh, yes you are. And at least *you're* here to play with me."

Leaning back on her elbows, Jillian stared up at the cottony clouds. An airplane flew by with a banner: "Jolly Roger—30th St. and Coastal Hwy." She studied each puffball, trying to decide what it looked like. One reminded her of a white rabbit with long ears, and another one looked like fluffy cotton candy. A cloud drifting into view reminded her of a lady's wide-brimmed straw hat, the kind her mother wore when they had their old time family photo taken on the boardwalk last summer.

Jillian had an idea. She propped herself up and began to make a lady in the sand. First, she formed her head, then her body and arms. With her finger, she traced a long, flowing dress and added feet. She mounded and patted a wide brimmed hat and tilted it slightly over her forehead. Then she added her sea treasures for her sand lady's features. Jillian used an oyster shell for her nose, two mussel shells for her eyes, and four razor clam shells for a happy, turned up smile. She placed a black skate's egg sac case in her sand lady's hand. Her mother once told her they were called lady's silk purses or *mermaid's purses*. It was black and bulb-like with little tails on all four corners. She found some dried sea grass and made her sand lady's hair.

She added two clear sea pebbles to each ear for earrings. They shimmered like real jewels. Next, she twisted three long stems of sea oat

Jillian making the Sand Lady.

grass and placed it around her sand lady's neck. In the middle of the necklace, she added a smooth, white, oval stone. Jillian discovered an orange day lily near the dune fence and snapped off the bloom. She arranged the flower on top of the wide brim of her floppy hat.

Sable stood and stretched her forelegs. She sniffed the sand lady and circled around her. Jillian sat on the back of her legs admiring her work of art.

"Isn't she pretty?" Jillian asked Sable.

Beyond the sand lady's hat, Jillian noticed a large, white feather left from a *snowy egret's* spring plumage. It was speared in a thicket of grasses near a dune fence. She knew to stay out of marked areas where threatened shorebird species such as *piping plovers* and *least terns* were nesting, and obeyed all refuge sign markers. Seeing no markers here, Jillian stuck her hand between two wooden slats and managed to grasp the feather. Twisting its quill back and forth, she admired the feather's natural beauty. It was a rare find. She brought the long, white feather back to her spot and tucked it on the right side of the lady's hat near the lily. It added a touch of elegance. There was something almost magical about the way it wisped in the sea breeze.

After her work, Jillian was so covered in sand she looked like a brown sugar doughnut. Jillian rose and stood above her sand lady with her hands on her hips. She liked the way her sand lady's hat was tilted slightly above her right eye. Her wispy, brown sea grass hair flattered her gem "stone" earrings and the minerals in the smooth stone pendant sparkled in the sun. Its oval shape reminded her of her grandmother's cameo locket.

Suddenly, the stone began to move! Jillian shook her head in disbelief and watched closely. It moved again! The stone rose as the sand lady drew her first breath. Then her head, chest, and arms came to life. Her breath came faster. The Sand Lady sat up and rubbed the sand from her eyes. Jillian stood in awe. There was a long silence. The gentle sea breeze lifted the Sand Lady's hat off her head, but she managed to catch it in time. She took off her hat and laid it beside her. From inside her silk

purse, she pulled out a beautiful, tortoise shell hair comb. With her delicate, ivory fingers, she twisted her long, brown hair and fastened it up with the comb. Then she firmly tugged on her straw hat and smiled at her maker. Jillian offered her hand to help the Sand Lady to her feet.

Her eyes were as blue as the sea and sparkled like pools of water. Her hands were as white and soft as the sand. With one firm pull, the elegant lady stood tall and brushed the sand from her mutton sleeves and long, white, cotton dress. She smiled graciously at Jillian. Her pale, pink mouth was as perfect as a bow. She didn't speak a word. Her beauty and actions spoke for her. Sable's ears fell back, and she growled at the Sand Lady. Then she sniffed her dainty feet. The dog sensed her kindness and licked her salty hand. Sable's soft, wet kiss tickled the Sand Lady, and she giggled with delight.

The Victorian beauty shaded her eyes with one hand and turned her head. From shore to sea and up and down the beach, she looked around in all directions. She hiked up her dress and walked toward the water. With each stride, her *pantaloons* showed slightly. Jillian walked with her to the firm sand at the high tide line, while Sable waited obediently at the secret thinking spot.

They padded in the moist sand toward the ocean. Jillian lifted her legs high and charged into the waves. Sea foam peaked on her thighs and decorated her legs like whipped meringue. The Sand Lady rolled up her mutton sleeves and hiked up her dress and *petticoats.* The cool surf made her shrill with delight. Her heels sank deep into the sand as she watched the rushing tide wash over her bare feet. A beautiful peach and blue marbled *whelk* shell rushed from the surf near her. It seemed to come as a gift. The Sand Lady grabbed it from the undertow and rinsed it in the salt water. It was a perfect shell. There wasn't a chip on it from churning in the sea. She held it close to her ear and listened to the ocean. It echoed memories of yesteryears. She closed her eyes and smiled peacefully. Jillian asked to see the beautiful shell. She held it tightly to her ear and listened to the roar of the ocean.

Jillian holding the shell to her ear, listening to the ocean.

10

OLD OCEAN CITY

The Sand Lady wrapped her arms around Jillian's small waist. In one quick but gentle swoop, she lifted her from the beach, and together they flew offshore. Their feet skimmed the foamy, white caps of sea crests and salt water misted their faces. Jillian looked down fearfully at the choppy water. She clutched the Sand Lady's arms and held on tightly. Straight ahead was the horizon of the clear, blue sky and the rough, gray sea. Beneath the water's surface, she could see the shadows of schools of flounder and bluefish. Jillian squeezed the lady's arms and looked up at her. A stream of water ran from the brim of the Sand Lady's hat. She began to feel safe locked in her embrace. She held on firmly and looked straight ahead into the wind. A school of dolphins leapt in unison ahead of them. Faster and faster they traveled across the ocean like a racing speedboat. The whir of the trade winds drowned out the loudest seabird calls. Squinting her eyes, Jillian could finally see a shoreline. One last breaker brought them near a fishing pier at a seaside resort town. At that moment, Jillian looked down at her wet tee shirt and found herself dressed in a blue top and skirt with bathing stockings. She was quite surprised by her costume. By the time Jillian got over the shock of this discovery, she and the Sand Lady had landed.

The two of them stood on the pier.

"Where are we?" Jillian asked.

Finally, the Sand Lady spoke. "We've gone back in time almost a hundred years to the seaside town where my family summered, 'Old Ocean City, Maryland'," she answered softly.

"Ding, Ding, Ding," rang the bell of the Baltimore, Chesapeake & Atlantic Railway steam engine as it chugged into the beach resort town from Division Street and came to a squeaky halt. Passengers of all shapes and sizes pushed forward off the train and to the station. Women donning floppy hats carried beach bags stuffed with towels, drinks, and snacks. Within arms' reach, children shuffled along toting tin sand pails with shovels, toy sailboats, and other favorite water toys. One strong fellow awkwardly carried a beach umbrella and a heavy, straw picnic basket that looked like it could feed an army. The *day-trippers* had all come for a day at the beach. Hotel porters waited to carry luggage for guests who had reservations at hotels, including the *Atlantic Hotel* and the *Plimhimmon.*

"*Bath houses*! Clean swimsuits for rent!" one attendant called from Showell's Bathhouses.

At eleven o'clock, the bathing hour was well underway. The sweaty day-trippers pressed their way to the row of bathhouses closest to the beach.

Jillian giggled. She covered her mouth and thought, *How silly they look!* Men in heavy woolen, black pullover shirts with big white "S's" on them and knee length trousers departed from the bathhouses. At Showell's, vacationers could rent a swimsuit and a locker for twenty-five cents a day. Three ladies in baggy tops and long skirts trekked down to the beach, ready to hit the surf. Families trudged through the hot sand to claim a cool, breezy spot near the high tide line, while others gathered around the swimming pool watching swimmers dive for coins. Men propped open wooden recliners and staked their beach umbrellas as ladies spread their blankets under tents. The white sand was dotted with bathers in dark swimsuits. A young fellow carried a pine surfboard and headed for the waves.

Young women chased runaway toddlers on the beach, while others snoozed under shady beach umbrellas. A brass band near a pavilion was playing a waltz, and swimmers bobbed up and down over the breakers to the rhythm of the faint music. Their clothes floated with air pockets as they kicked their legs.

Showell's Locker Key

Beach bathers at Plimhimmon Hotel.

Again, the Sand Lady spoke. Her voice was soft and sweet. "Would you like to swim?" she asked.

Jillian warmly answered, "Yes, and you can call me Jillian."

Side by side with their hands linked, the two time travelers bathed knee-deep in the surf. Jillian followed the Sand Lady's lead and bobbed in rhythm with the other people. *What fun!* she thought. They laughed giddily like little children, trying just to keep their balance in the rough surf. Next, the band led into a rousing march by John Philip Sousa. Holding hands, they jumped to and fro over the shallow breakers. The music ended as quickly as it had begun.

Refreshed from the water, the two of them headed for the boardwalk. They passed by *surfmen* launching a surfboat for a ship rescue drill. Hand in hand, they weaved their way through the vacationers relaxing on the beach. One family enjoyed a ride along the beach on an oxendrawn cart.

The boardwalk was a clamor of sights, sounds, and smells. The aroma of chocolate, fudge, and salt water taffy wafted from the candy store door. At Dolle's, one young man stirred a batter of hot, gooey, caramel popcorn. Its sweet smell made Jillian's mouth water.

"Ice cream! Ice cream!" one vendor in white shouted from the Sugar Bowl.

As the Sand Lady and Jillian were walking past, a man with the bushy mustache and slicked back hair leaned forward in his ice cream booth, waved to them, and said with a warm smile, "You two look like you could use some ice cream. What do you say?"

The Sand Lady held up two fingers and ordered, "We'll each have two scoops of vanilla, please."

Then she opened her silk purse and paid the man with some change. Jillian reached for her double dipper sugar cone. It had speckles of *real* vanilla bean. Twisting her cone, she licked all sides to catch the sweet drippings. They found a boardwalk bench to enjoy their treat.

Dolle's Candyland.

14

Further down the boardwalk was a *millinery* shop. Pressing her nose and fingertips against the glass, Jillian peered through the display window seeing hats, hats, and more hats! There were sun bathing hats and bonnets, hats for promenading the boardwalk, and hats for afternoon tea. At that moment, the Sand Lady and Jillian looked at each other. Giving an agreeable nod, they entered the shop to browse.

What a heyday they had trying on hats and striking poses in the full-length, gold etched mirror! There wasn't a hat in the shop they missed. Even the merchant enjoyed his cheerful customers.

"Wait, I just received a new shipment of summer hats from New York today. Perhaps one of those will suit you," he offered.

He slipped into the back of the store and brought out a stack of hatboxes. The salesman untied the pink satin bow from the top box and presented the white hat to his customers. It had a pink silk ribbon around the brim and egret feathers. Jillian and the Sand Lady were awed at the stunning hat. Just for fun, Jillian tried it on. She looked in the mirror. As she thought, the hat was too big for her.

The Sand Lady smiled, "We'll take it."

He placed the hat back inside the box, but the Sand Lady stopped him, "No need for that. I think she'll wear it now"

She fitted it on Jillian's head as snugly as it would go and then paid the merchant. Jillian was tickled with her new hat. She felt so grown up and Victorian, like the Sand Lady.

"You ladies have a nice day and enjoy your vacation. Come see us again," he said cheerfully.

Outside of the millinery shop door, the Sand Lady clutched Jillian's small hand. Two boys on bicycles rambled passed them. The bathing hour was well over, and the boardwalk was bustling with activity. Couples holding hands strolled by, pausing to window-shop at the Popular Doll Place and other novelty stores. Women donned parasols in the late day sun. Hotel guests rocked on porch fronts and terraces, enjoying the sea view as they sipped on their afternoon tea or Moxie, a popular soft drink.

At Conner's restaurant, a waiter served them two cups of hot English tea. Jillian dunked her butter cookie in her tea. Mimicking the Sand Lady, she daintily held her china teacup, extended her pinky, and sipped her tea. For a while, they enjoyed each other's company as they watched the crowds promenade the boardwalk. What great sport!

From a nearby window, they could hear the deep voices and laughter of gentlemen playing cards and the popular game of chess. The stench of cigars drifted from the window behind them. They rolled their eyes, wrinkled up their noses, and finished their tea.

"How about one last stroll on the boardwalk?" the Sand Lady suggested.

Jillian wiped the corners of her mouth with her linen napkin and placed it on the table. The Sand Lady slipped a bill under her saucer and followed her off the porch.

15

Atlantic Hotel.

Horse carriages shared the road with some "horseless carriages" or autos. The horses' clippity-clop made a merry sound.

The Sand Lady gently pulled Jillian's hand, "I'll show you horses *we* can ride."

They picked up their pace, passing by beautiful hotels and Victorian-style cottages. Some hotels, like *The Atlantic,* were grand with many rooms and windows, and *verandahs,* or porches with enough rockers for every guest. Jillian could hear the faint, familiar sound of merry-go-round music. They shuffled and weaved their way through the crowd, straight to the carousel ponies at Trimper's Luna Park in Windsor Resorts. The ride was getting ready to start. What luck! Two animals were left. The Sand Lady flung her silk purse around her ostrich's long neck, and then she helped Jillian mount her white horse. Before the ride started, Jillian reached back to touch her horse's tail. It was made of *real* horsehair. She felt the carved ridges in his mane and the pink roses on her horse's shoulder. Jillian thought it was the prettiest animal on the carousel.

"Hold onto the brass pole with two hands!" the Sand Lady shouted gaily.

Then she mounted her ostrich sidesaddle and the organ began to play. Up and down and round and round, they rode. They passed the same blurred crowd over and over again and listened to the organ music. Jillian remembered the old-fashioned carousel at the amusement park near her home. It had been a while since she had been on a merry-go-round, and it felt especially wonderful!

On their way back to the pier, they stopped for some ice cold lemonade and Cracker Jack. The Sand Lady tried her skill at the basketball shoot. She tried to win an Oriental doll for Jillian, but only shot "rimmers."

Further down the boardwalk was a photography studio. A poster in the window advertised "Picture Postcards." A few day-trippers were waiting in line to have their picture taken in front of a beach backdrop scene. The camera flashed brightly in their faces. Jillian tugged on the Sand Lady's arm, coaxing her to have their picture taken. They waited their turn in line and watched

Carousel Horse

how the photographer posed each customer, then stood behind a black camera to snap their photo. With her delicate fingers, the Sand Lady combed and arranged Jillian's hair and placed her hat back on her head. It was their turn next. What a pretty picture they took together! Their eyes sparkled and their faces glowed from a day of sun. It was an eventful day and their real photo card showed it. They stood and admired the picture together. Then, the Sand Lady paid the clerk and slipped the photo card in her silk purse.

TIME TO GO

By late afternoon, a cool breeze was beginning to blow, and clouds were billowing up over the sun. After a quick bite to eat on the boardwalk, the sun-tired day-trippers packed up and boarded the last train back on the Baltimore, Chesapeake & Atlantic Railway.

The conductor cupped his hands around his mouth.

"All aboard! All aboard!" he called.

Last minute vacationers rushed to catch the train with their bags stuffed with popcorn, salt-water taffy, fans, shell dish prizes, and other souvenirs. The slow grinding of gears started up and the steam engine chugged westward.

The Sand Lady smacked an early evening mosquito on her ankle. It was then she realized they had best be getting back while there was still daylight left. Hand in hand, they walked down the fishing pier passing by shops they visited earlier. When they reached the end of the pier, Jillian looked back over her shoulder. She could see the twin *turrets* of the Windsor Hotel and a magnificent Ferris wheel. Colorful awnings, banners, and flags trimmed the stores and hotels on the boardwalk.

At the very end of the island city, Jillian could see the fishing shacks. Earlier that day she watched the men *pound net fish*. Teams of fishermen pulled in nets full of trout, porgies, hardheads or croakers, and flounder. Vacationers looked on as two horse teams hauled their catch off the beach. Fishermen sorted them in slatted baskets and they were iced in barrels to be sold to restaurant buyers on the dock.

Baltimore, Chesapeake and Atlantic Railroad.

Pound Net Fishermen.

As quickly as they came, the Sand Lady whisked Jillian away over the ocean. Streamers of pink and purple clouds trailed across the sky. The sun was still an orange ball, but was dropping quickly over the Bay.

Jillian gripped the Sand Lady's arms and looked straight ahead. The ocean loomed endlessly. A strong crosswind lifted her hat from her head.

She gasped.

"My hat, my hat!" Jillian cried.

Jillian felt it lift from her head as she touched her head. It was too late. Her new hat was lost to the sea.

It was dusk when they returned to the hidden secret thinking spot near the crepe myrtle in her backyard. Jillian glanced down and noticed she was wearing her oversized tee shirt again. There was a long silence as they caught their breaths and collected themselves from the journey. The Sand Lady removed the tortoise shell comb from her hair. She pulled out the long strands of brown hair from the comb and twisted it into a small ringlet, or *hair lock.*

"I would like you to have this," she said.

Jillian clutched the hair ringlet in her palm.

"Now turn around and I'll put this comb in your hair."

Jillian turned around, and felt the Sand Lady twisting her sun-streaked brown hair. She spiraled it into a bun and tightly inserted the comb.

"There," she said. "Now don't lose it. You have such beautiful hair."

Jillian felt the tight bun and the firm fit of the comb. When she turned around, the Sand Lady was gone!

"Come back, come back!" Jillian cried.

She called over and over again but it was no use. Her eyes darted to the sand sculpture. It was still there. Every piece of gem "stone" and the hat with the day lilies was still intact…everything but the egret feather. Jillian felt sad. She didn't even have a chance to say goodbye, or to thank her for the gift. She felt a sense of "aloneness" and sat in the sand for a long time.

Seeking comfort, she squatted next to Sable and asked her, "Where did she go? Where is my Sand Lady?"

Jillian crying with Sable

She squatted next to Sable and cradled her dog's head in her hands. Jillian scratched her behind the ears.

"And you waited for me all day. You must be thirsty."

Sable panted. A strong whiff of smelly, dead fish reached Jillian's nostrils.

She gagged, "You stinky dog! What have you gotten into?"

Laying like a sphinx, Sable held a dead crab between her two front paws. She rubbed her muzzle on the lifeless, gray shell.

Jillian scolded, "No!"

She shooed Sable away and buried the crab with her foot.

"Boy, wait 'til Mom and Dad get a whiff of you. You'll really be in the doghouse now. Bad girl!" she said.

Sable hung her black head low to the ground. She knew she was in trouble but she just couldn't help herself. Jillian didn't blame her either. After all, a dog is a dog. In a loving tone, she commanded her to heel. Sable walked meekly beside her.

On their way back to the house, Jillian thought about the events of her incredible trip with the Sand Lady. How she wished she could have spoken to her just one more time!

Back home, Jillian used the hose around the side of the house on Sable. Jillian held Sable by the collar and sprayed her face and front paws.

As she did, Jillian thought back to her whole experience, "It **must** have been the egret feather that brought her to life."

THE BEACH HOUSE

Jillian hooked Sable to the long lead line at the bottom of the deck steps. After lapping up a cool bowl of water, the tired lab retreated to her resting spot under the deck. Jillian slowly climbed the steps with one hand on the railing. From inside the front door, she could hear her Mom softly singing to a song on the radio as she put the finishing touches on her Fenwick Lighthouse painting. Jillian padded quietly into the room.

"Hi, Mom," she said softly.

Her mother paused, "Hey, Jilly, where have you been all day?"

Jillian entered the room and settled herself in the wicker chair. Before she could say a word about her day, her father was standing in the doorway rubbing his wet hair in a towel.

"Beth, have you seen my blue sweatshirt?" he asked in a muffled tone from under his towel.

"Check the dryer," she answered.

He looked up and saw Jillian.

"Hey, Jilly Willy, thought you were going to help me clean those fish today," he said.

Jillian replied wearily, "I was going to...guess I forgot."

"Well, you didn't miss your chance for a scaling lesson. I didn't clean them yet. It's been awful quiet around here today. Where've you been?"

He hung the towel around his neck and waited for her answer.

Jillian looked up at him from the chair. Already her adventure with the Sand Lady had begun to seem like something she dreamed about, and yet she knew it was real. She didn't know if she should say anything at all to her parents. Would they really believe her?

"Oh, nowhere," she sighed, "just out on the beach."

"Bet you're hungry," her dad said. "They'll have plenty of hot dogs and marshmallows at the bonfire tonight."

"Bonfire? What bonfire?" Jillian asked.

Her dad replied, "The community bonfire is tonight. I thought it would be fun for us to go. They're calling for meteor showers tonight, too. Why don't you wash up and find a sweatshirt?"

Jillian fought back a yawn, "Okay, I guess."

She was tired but at the same time, she was glad they were doing something as a family.

"And Jilly," her father added, "I like your hair up like that. It looks pretty."

Jillian reached back to feel her tortoise shell comb. Knowing it was still in there reassured her that her day **was** real.

Fenwick Island Lighthouse

QUALITY TIME

A cool shower was refreshing. Jillian washed and combed her sun-streaked hair. Then, she twisted it back into a bun and wore the comb. She tied a sweatshirt around her waist and rambled down the wooden steps to the kitchen. The three of them walked down the deck steps toward the beach. Her dad carried the heavy-duty flashlight and the blanket. Her mom shouldered a canvas bag packed with bug spray, marshmallows, graham crackers, and thick chocolate bars. Jillian walked between them, holding their spare hands. It was comforting being together as a family. She squeezed their hands tightly. It was a little game she liked to play with them. They would squeeze her hands back. A wide grin spread over her face. She finally had her parents all to herself!

Jillian snuggled under the plaid, wool blanket between her Mom and Dad. Other families sat around the fire with them, and everyone ate hot dogs and s'mores. There was always someone weaving a tale. Her father stood up to take his turn tending the fire. He draped the blanket on her shoulders and kissed her forehead. This moment reassured her of his love.

As Jillian watched the embers shoot from the crackling logs, she thought perhaps she bothered her parents too often about flying kites and other things she wanted when they had other things to do. She had never really thought of her parents as people with interests and hobbies. Just like she enjoyed her "alone" time in her secret thinking spot, they were entitled to their private moments to do whatever they wished. In the future, she thought she could practice a little more patience and understanding. Maybe she could develop a hobby of her own. After all, she was growing up, and her parents would be expecting more from her. She understood about quality time, and the bonfire was a memorable event for her family.

Jillian's adventure with the Sand Lady helped her not to be quite so dependent on her parents for her entertainment. She was suddenly struck with a new found appreciation for Ocean City. She was also eager to explore Ocean City's sites to see how much of Old Ocean City she and the Sand Lady had visited still remained today.

That evening, the children hunted for ghost crabs with their flashlights and were thrilled to see the shooting stars. One family even brought sparklers to share. That night, Jillian slept like a baby.

Bonfire

KITE DAY

Jillian's father twisted the mini-blinds open.

"Time to get up, sleepyhead. It's almost eleven o'clock. Thought we might go take a look at some kites on the boardwalk, so get dressed and come down for brunch," he said cheerfully.

Her mom made fried egg and bacon sandwiches. It was a quiet meal. Sable sat like a black lab statue, waiting for someone to feel sorry for her and give her a bite of toast crust. She never gave up until everyone had finished the last bite. On this morning, no one saved a bite for her. She barked sharply and backed into the kitchen cabinets, just to let everyone know she didn't get her share.

"That dog has some strong personality," her mother said as she gave her a cup of dry dog food.

Jillian drank the rest of her orange juice and helped her mother with the dishes. She rinsed the plates and stacked them in the dishwasher while her mother wiped the counter and stove. Still, she didn't tell them about her Sand Lady. She didn't quite know where to begin.

Her father entered the kitchen, jingling his keys.

He asked Beth, "Do you know of anyone who might want to buy a kite today?"

Jillian turned her head, "I do! I do!" she answered excitedly.

The three of them piled into their jeep and headed down Ocean Highway for the boardwalk.

Choosing a kite was quite an ordeal. The store was stocked with kites of all shapes and sizes. Jillian settled on a ladybug kite. Before they left the boards, Jillian's dad had to have his boardwalk favorite: salty French fries with malt vinegar. Jillian and her mother enjoyed a custard on one of the boardwalk benches.

That afternoon, the three of them assembled and flew the fancy kite. Her father showed her how to make the kite tail swoop low then rise high again.

"Tighten up on your string, Jill," her Dad instructed.

Jillian wrapped the twine up as fast as she could, but it was too late. Her ladybug kite took a dive into the dunes.

"That's par for the course," her dad said, "You'll get the hang of it. It just takes practice, Jilly."

Jillian stood in the sand and shielded her eyes from the sun. She squinted. It looked as if her kite crashed near her secret spot. The three of them walked toward the crash landing site. It was then that she decided to share her sand sculpture with her parents.

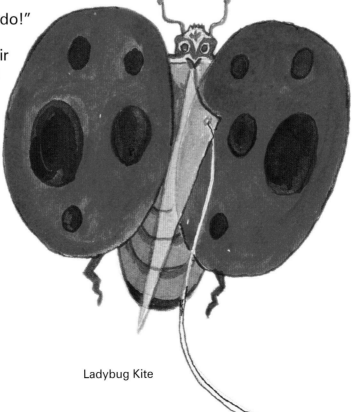

Ladybug Kite

23

LOST TO THE SEA

On the way, Jillian told them of how she made her own Sand Lady yesterday. How she decorated her with shells, sea grass, and day lilies. Then she told them how she came to life when she tucked the egret feather in her hat. She rattled on and on about how they took a trip across the ocean and about all of the fun they had together. Her parents stood amused and looked at each other. They refrained from laughing or even smirking at their daughter's wild imagination.

"Come and see! Come and see!" she cried.

Jillian sprinted ahead of them. Her parents followed her to her private thinking spot. She pointed to where her sand lady was, but she was gone. The tide had washed her away. Her dried brown sea grass hair had rolled into the dune grasses like tumbleweed. A few scattered shells were left and the skate's egg sac was half-buried in the tidal sand.

"My Sand Lady! She's gone!" Jillian cried.

Her parents could see that the Sand Lady had been very **real** to their daughter. Jillian felt a sudden sense of loss. She wasn't ready to lose her Sand Lady to Mother Nature and thought she would at least be around a few days longer. She bent down to pick up the few remaining gem "stones" and lady's purse. She stood up and cradled them in her shirt.

Richard saw tears welling up in his daughter's blue eyes. He understood how she felt and put his arm around her shoulders. Then she realized her tortoise shell hair comb was the only solid piece of evidence that was left. Jillian turned the back of her head to show her parents.

"See my comb? See it? She gave it to me before she left," Jillian said.

Her parents were glad their daughter had such a creative imagination. Richard nudged Beth with his elbow.

Audubon Book.

24

Jillian wearing the hair comb, admiring her reflection
in a gold-etched Victorian mirror.

"She takes after you, Beth," he said softly.

For a few moments, they stood consoling their daughter. Her father managed to salvage the ladybug kite. After he rolled up the twine, they went inside.

Jillian always treasured that comb. As years passed, Jillian wore the comb on special occasions. It was quite becoming on her and made her look older ... more mature. She had a beautiful face. The comb flattered her blonde summer highlights and her big, blue eyes. Jillian had pressed the ringlet of brown hair she received between the pages of her Audubon book, next to the snowy egret picture. Her parents saw that summer as a milestone year of girlhood for their daughter.

As a girl and young woman, Jillian made many more sand ladies and decorated them the same way, with shells, sea grass, and beach stones. None of them were magical like her first Sand Lady ... the one who wore the egret feather in her hat.

GLOSSARY

Atlantic Hotel – the first large hotel built in Ocean City in 1875. The railroad ran in front of the hotel on Baltimore Avenue.

bath house – small buildings on the beach where vacationers could rent swimsuits and towels for the day. Showell's and Rayne's were two popular bathhouses.

day-trippers – vacationers from cities such as Baltimore and Washington who took the railroad to coastal area resorts.

Diamondback Terrapin – the state reptile of Maryland. They have diamond-shaped rings on their upper shells. In the nineteenth century the turtle was harvested as a gourmet food in stew. Now they are protected by the Department of Natural Resources.

hair lock – In Victorian times, women would save their strands of hair and make ringlets for extra curls on a wig. They treasured hair locks as a special remembrance of someone they loved.

least tern – an endangered and protected shorebird with forked tails and slender wings, native to the Atlantic Coast.

mermaid's purse – a bulb-like, black object with four pointed tails. It is the egg case of a skate. It is also called a lady's silk purse.

pantaloons – long, frilly pants worn under a dress or skirt.

Eastern Bluebird.

Baltimore Oriole.

pavilion – a roofed building where outdoor summer concerts were held at the shore.

petticoat – an undergarment worn in layers like slips under skirts or dresses.

piping plover – an endangered and protected shorebird with long pointed wings, native to the Atlantic Coast and found on mud flats and beaches.

Plimhimmon Hotel – The "Plim" was built in 1893 by Rosalie Shreve. It was destroyed by the fire in 1962 and rebuilt in 1969. The peak of the hotel tower was saved in the fire.

pound net fishing – a method of fishing popular from 1900 through the 1920s. Teams of fishermen hauled in nets filled with schools of fish. Horses would pull the loads of fish to shore. The fish were iced in barrels and sold to restaurant owners and fish markets at the dock.

snowy egret – a white shorebird with a thin black bill and black feet. It feeds in shallow waters and mud flats.

surfboat – a boat used to rescue mariners from a sinking ship. Surf men pulled the boat to the scene of the shipwreck mounted on its carriage with wheels.

surfmen – a crew of six watermen whose mission was to save the lives of the shipwrecked along the coastline. They lived in a lifesaving station with a keeper appointed by the government. The lifesaving station was once on Caroline Street but has been moved to the boardwalk and is now a museum.

turret – a cone-shaped roof like the two on the Windsor Hotel.

veranda – (also spelled verandah) a large porch on an inn or hotel.

OLD OCEAN CITY

TIMELINE

1875 – The Wicomico and Pocomoke Railroad built an extension line from Berlin with a bridge across the Sinexpuxent Bay. The Atlantic Hotel opens with 400 rooms.

1878 – The Ocean City Life Station was first built at Caroline Street. In 1977, it was moved to the end of the boardwalk and is now a museum.

1893 – The Plimhimmon Hotel was built by Rosalie Shrieve.

1894 – The Wicomico and Pocomoke Railroad became the Baltimore, Chesapeake and Atlantic Railroad.

1896 – The Showells moved to Ocean City and built the Oceanic Hotel, The Blue Lattice Tearoom, and Showell's Bath House and Theater. They also built the first swimming pool in Ocean City.

1900 – Daniel Trimper built Luna Park. The whip, the Ferris wheel, and the merry-go-round were popular rides.

1905 – Rudolph Dolle, a candy maker from New York, opened his business on the pier.

1907 – The Fishing Pier project was completed.

1912 – A permanent boardwalk is built. Trimper Amusements opened as Windsor Resorts. Its carousel is the oldest continuously operating carousel in the United States.

1915 – City Hall was built by the State Department of Education as a training place for teachers.

1920 – Ocean City's first firehouse was built. Pound net fishing became a popular fishing method through the 1920s.

1925 – A big fire burned the Fishing Pier, a section of the boardwalk, and the Atlantic Hotel.

1933 – Part of Luna Park was washed away in the big storm.

This is a partial timeline of Old Ocean City to help the reader understand the setting and the events in the story.

BIBLIOGRAPHY

Corddry, Mary. *City on the Sand, Ocean City, Maryland and the People Who Built It*. Centreville, Maryland: Tidewater Press, 1991.

DeVincent-Hayes, Nan, Jacob, and John. *Images of America, Ocean City Volume I*. Charlestown, South Carolina: Arcadia Publishing, 1999.

Gaskins, Edgar. *Yesteryears, A Bit of Ocean City History and Heritage*. Self-published paperback.

Hurley, George and Suzanne. *Ocean City, Maryland, A Pictorial History*. Virginia Beach, Virginia: Donning Company Publishers, 1991.

Kyle, Mary Pat. *Fenwick Island, Ice Age to Jet Age*. Fenwick Island, Delaware: published by the author, 1995.

Lencek, Lena and Gideon Bosker. *The Beach: The History of Paradise on Earth*. New York, New York: Penguin Putnam, Inc., 1998.

Life-Saving Station

Photo of Corinne & Bari

ABOUT THE AUTHOR

Corinne M. Litzenberg is a native Marylander and has lived in Cecil County, Maryland, all of her life. Since childhood, she has spent many summer vacations in Ocean City. She remembers when her family rented rafts on the beach and strolled on the boards to eat boardwalk food for a special family night out for dinner. They were allowed to pick and choose what they wanted to eat that night. Boardwalk fries and ice cream were always on the list of favorites. Corinne is also the author of *The Sand Lady: A Cape May Tale*, and a children's book series, *Flock Tales from the Flats*, which teaches about waterfowl conservation on the Chesapeake Bay. A graduate of the Tome School, Dr. Litzenberg earned a B.S. from the University of Delaware, an M.Ed. from Loyola College of Baltimore, and an Ed.D. from Wilmington College, where her dissertation focused on local environmental education. She presents programs to children and adults on the writing process and local culture, and teaches second grade at Elk Neck Elementary, a Green School in Cecil County, Maryland. Corinne has two children, Todd and Natalie. She likes to read and learn about our country's history and is a member of the Daughters of the American Revolution.

About the Illustrator

Inspired by local architecture and rich landscapes, Delaware artist Bari A. Edwards prefers the difficult medium of watercolor because of its translucent quality that defines and enhances her many subjects. Among Bari's favorite childhood memories were the days spent with her family along the Jersey shore from Atlantic City and Barnegat Light to Long Beach Island. Collaborating with Corinne on *The Sand Lady* has been an incredible opportunity and natural progression to widen her artistic horizons.

Bayside Sunset.